To my loving husband and children who mean the world to me and inspire everything I do.

- Caroline Peters

www.mascotbooks.com

For more information, please contact:
Mascot Books
560 Herndon Parkway #120
Herndon, VA 20170
info@mascotbooks.com

CPSIA Code: PRT0613A
ISBN-10: 1620862727
ISBN-13: 9781620862728

Printed in the United States

NEW YORK CITY

Caroline Peters
illustrated by James Balkovek

A is for the Big Apple
The nickname for this city,
Come and explore with me
It will be so fun and pretty!

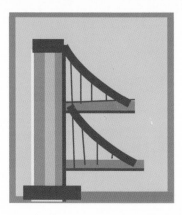

B is for the Brooklyn Bridge
Stretching over the East River.
A famous icon of New York
A spectacular view it will deliver.

C is for Carnegie Hall
Let's go listen to some music.
A concert will be awesome…
The venue has got great acoustics!

D is for Doll!
Go pick out your favorite one!
The American Girl Store is the place
It simply cannot be outdone.

E is for Empire State Building
Of great stature and height.
Get a view from the observation deck
It is an incredible sight.

F is for FAO Schwartz
This toy store can't be beat.
Buy books, toys, games, and trains
Or candy that tastes so sweet!

G is for the Giants
This is New York's football team.
Head over to the stadium
To jump, cheer, and scream!

H is for Horse-Drawn Carriage
To trot you around Central Park.
Snuggle up and enjoy the scenery
During the day or when it's dark.

I is for Ice Cream
A refreshing, cool treat.
Enjoy it on a summer day.
It's the best way to beat the heat!

ICE
CREAM

J is for Jugglers
You might see one on the street.
Entertainment is all around
You never know who you might meet.

K is for the Kicks of the RocKettes
known for their precision dance.
Their high kicks are spectacular
Watch them leap, tap, and prance.

ROCKETTES

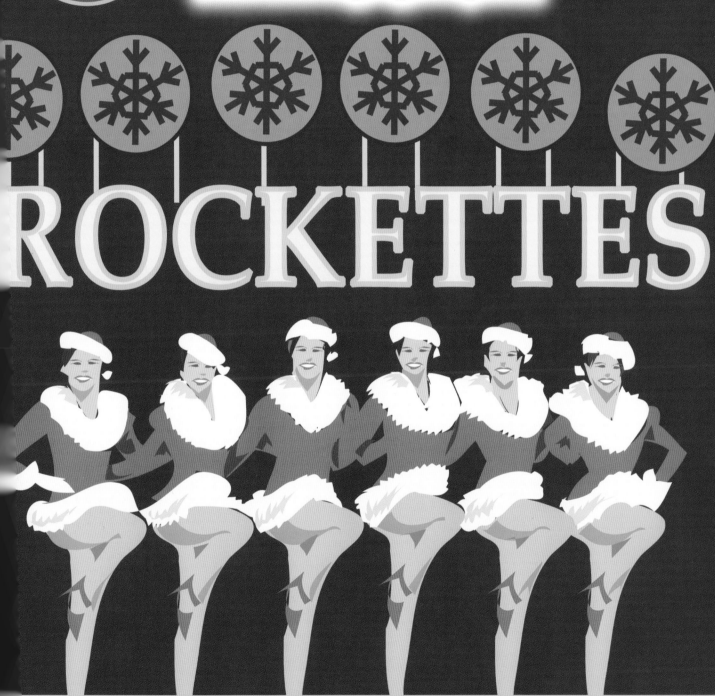

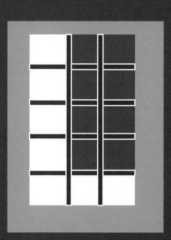

L is for Lights Lights Lights
They shine so brilliant and bright.
This city is always alive
Rain or shine, day or night.

M is for Musicals
On Broadway, you can see
Acting, singing, and dancing.
Catch one, two, or three!

N is for New York Firefighters
So courageous and brave.
They are the finest in the land.
Many lives, they save.

O is for Occasion
What brings you to town?
For me, it is the grand hotels
They never let you down.

P is for Pizza
The most famous in the land.
You'll find it on every street corner.
Pizza here is in high demand!

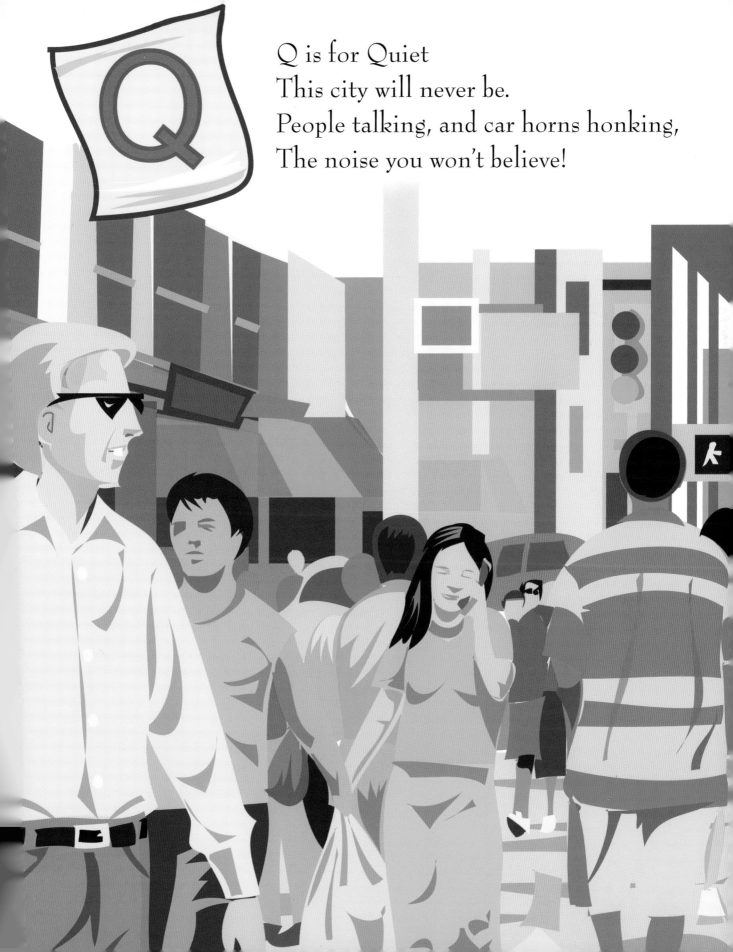

Q is for Quiet
This city will never be.
People talking, and car horns honking,
The noise you won't believe!

R is for Rockefeller Center
Put on your hats and gloves
It is time to go ice skating
While we stare at the skyscrapers above.

S is for the Statue of Liberty
A symbol of freedom for the U.S.
Let's take a ferry over to see it.
This country is truly blessed!

T is for Times Square
The ball drops here on New Year's Eve.
See the enormous electric signs
We won't ever want to leave!

U is for Universities
The City is home to many schools:
Columbia, NYU, and St. John's.
Studying here would be so cool!

V is for Villages
Greenwich, East, and West.
I like them all…
Which one do you like the best?

W is for Water
It tends to rain a lot.
Be sure to bring an umbrella
Without one, you don't want to be caught.

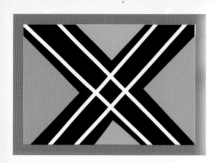

X is for eXcellent
The best time it will be
Exploring this fast-paced city
Because there is so much to see!

Y is for New York Yankees
This baseball team you'll love.
Come to the Bronx with me
But don't forget your glove!

Z is for Zzzzz
So tired you will be.
After a day in the Big Apple
Lots of sleep you will need!

Traveling with you was so much fun!
We learned a lot and saw New York City glow.
If you'd like to take another trip,
My twin brother, Michael, will show you Colorado!

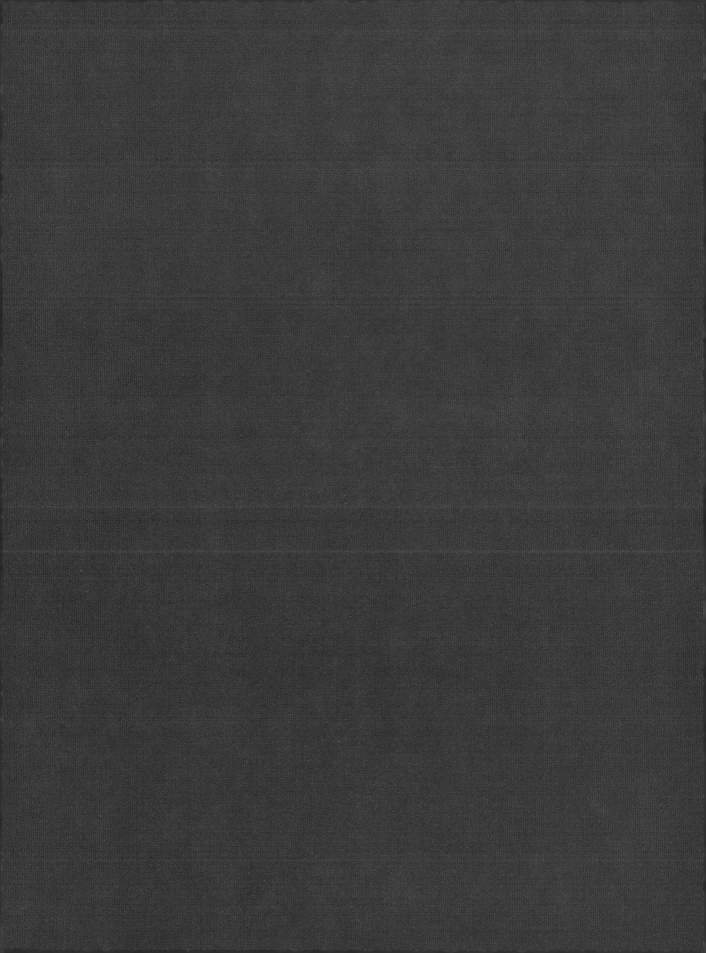

About the Author

Caroline Peters graduated from the University of Texas in Austin. She currently lives in Houston with her husband and three children. She is a former kindergarten teacher and continues to have a passion for teaching young children. An avid traveler, she was inspired to create an alphabet series to help make teaching fun!